TALKING TO CROWS

TALKING TO

CROWS

STEFAN T. WONG

Rockrose Press

An imprint of AUTHORS WHO LEAD™
ROCKROSEPRESS.COM

Paperback ISBN: 9781954801677
Hardcover with Dust Jacket ISBN: 9781954801691
Case Laminate Hardcover ISBN: 9781954801684
eBook ISBN: 9781954801707

FIC019000 FICTION / Literary
FIC039000 FICTION / Visionary & Metaphysical

Cover design and typesetting by Kaitlin Barwick

stefantwong.com

To those who wish to be.
For my little sunbeam.

CONTENTS

THE INVITATION   1
PROEM   3

I.   A CHILD   7

II.   THE TEACHER   11

III.   THE DOORS   19

IV.   THE WAY OF CREATION   27

V.   THE WAY OF MYSTERIES   35

VI.   THE WAY OF GROWTH   45

VII.   THE WAY OF CURIOSITY   53

VIII.   THE WAY OF THE UNTAMED   61

IX.   THE WAY OF LIBERATION   71

X.   THE WAY OF FLIGHT   81

XI.   THE WAY OF POWER   91

XII.   THE WAY OF YOU   101

XIII.   THE WHISPERS   109

EPILOGUE – THE WIND   117

FLOWERS   130
ABOUT THE AUTHOR   134

We have such potential.
Not the potential to be something,
but the potential to be.

THE INVITATION

I hope you reawaken to yourself. I hope you see each way you take as a path and discover that no path is a mistake but a way.

The world exists and will exist. Systems are and will be established. Processes do and will control behavior. There will be times of plenty and times of less. Life will begin and life will end.

But we are not required to be controlled or manipulated by the things around us. What happens to us does not have to take root. The decisions we make in a moment do not have to define. And we do not merely need to exist.

I do not know *the* path. I do not know *the* way. But I believe each of us has within us the power to experience our own life, to experience our self in our fullness.

If you go beyond this page, perhaps you are open or perhaps you are willing to be open. Open to doing more than existing in your lifetime. Open to experiencing every moment with which you are blessed. Open to full self-discovery. Open to being who and what you are in the midst of the happenings of this world.

Just as each way flows in its time and significance, so too do the passages within these pages. Moving from the first to the last passage may be the way for some. For others it may be choosing a passage based on how one feels rather than the order in which the passage appears. Just as one should in life, choose the way as felt best for your journey.

I do not believe you are here by happenstance, you found this, and this found you. I believe you are here for the reminding of you.

PROEM

On a mile's hike to school, the child comes across majestic black birds. The birds sing a sweet song that the child feels. They're far off, but feel a part of him.

"They're speaking to you," whispers the wise mother. "Go ahead, talk back."

With joy and wonder, the boy sings the same song of the birds.

Call and response on a mile's journey. The birds keep the child company and give the child comfort as he journeys alone to school. Even when the child was too tired or too dismayed, there the birds stayed.

The birds' sweet melody was salve to the child. A nectar to a bitter earth. A comfort in the wild. And though the mother could not travel with him each day, her gift remained all the same. Her wise counsel granted him the protection and guidance of the majestic black birds. Her opening the senses of the child and the channel between worlds promised the child and birds grew as one.

Guardians became they. Teachers they would stay. Majestic teachings from the teachers of the sky teaching of the way. And though he may not recognize the moment in time it happened, the Source from whence they all came had cemented the connection.

The child would grow and live life. He'd learn things in this place. This place, this plain, would open to him in different ways and he'd experience whatever it displayed.

He matriculated through systems. He played a part. All the while the teachings from the teachers never left. He always struggled with feeling a part. He struggled with understanding purpose. And his care for the same was never quite there.

Although see them the child no longer could, the majestic birds' song always sang in his heart. Being was his nature, not playing a part.

One day the now man-child was blatantly reminded of his ancient teachers, and the vibration of their song in his heart one like no other creature. He had not realized that in all this time, he'd forgotten.

He'd forgotten simplicity's beauty. He'd forgotten the wonder of life without trade. He'd simply forgotten, forgotten his way. Wrapped in a numbing pattern. Pushed by an invisible force. The man-child was not influenced but manipulated to take a course.

But the wise song. Oh, the wise song remained. And even if he couldn't remember the name, it carried him all the same. The man-child had walked the teachings. The man-child had lived the song. The majestic black birds had embedded the magic of being deep in his soul. The connection to the source that the wise mother had nurtured remained unbroken even through the quiet noise to which he subjected.

Now the man-child attempts to preserve the song taught to him from the greatest teachers he has ever known. The song that stretches to the outermost parts of the universe of the soul. The song sang to him opening a channel to the Source. The song that protects and guides him daily so to live without remorse.

The song the beautiful crows called to the man-child was the song he now sees as a teaching to effortlessly be. Each person maintains a different path to being, hopefully the learnings of this path will reawaken another to what they have known all along. The knowing that that person is capable of beautifully being. And from that being, worlds of fulfillment and discovery await.

May we all be a stream of the ocean. Connected to and a manifestation of the Source.

I

A CHILD

And there was a time when presence existed.
Beauty, natural. Love, boundless.

A mother, a father, a child. Existed. Nothing in hand but the love of each other.

Her hair shimmered long black and coiled. Her voice soothed, taming demons and freeing souls. Her gold-kissed skin was a wonder. She lived in a different time and space but held in heart the love for any. Separate and apart she would make her journey. No matter the cost. With only one in sight. Freedom.

His courage vibrated. His mind sharp. Rich as the coffea liberica his skin shown amongst the paling reality. Journeying to and fro as he decided, he was a presence, a force. He would move in challenge, and he would speak the language of audacity. A comfort to the margins, a viper to the captor. Only one in sight. Freedom.

A child . . .

He treads and he dares. Under the moonlit sky the dust seeming specks of silver blessing his every movement. Moving with such poetic grace, the dust dances on the air. Swirls here, lifting there, circling hence, and kissing thence.

The night was a child's home. Seeing all manner of creation. Dancing to rhythms unheard. Feeling the undisturbed energies. There, a child was natural. There, resided a power. Walking gingerly, the mother and father guided, held, and nurtured a child, where resided the power into the waking hour.

A child walked the road with the wise mother. Together they greeted the dawnings of the day. Free to run to and fro, laugh high and low, and learn from the wise mother without thought, a child bellowed in the morning dew.

II

THE TEACHER

I have been there to help the universe unfold.
Sharing when the waters receded.

A messenger to the gods
to determine what was needed.

One with all creation.
A part of how it was seeded.

Enlightenment is a path open
to all who are open and who heed it.

The sky was heavy. Conformity.
The stench strong. Fear.
This world slowing. Limitation.

Its origin unclear. A creation with the ability to transcend life
and death. A god or goddess wielding the power of war.
An embodiment of every color and hue in the universe.
A caretaker of wisdom. Wisdom itself.

Whatever its origin, it is.
And in its being it knows.
And in its knowing it sees.
In its sight it shows.

The Heavens were never quite the same without its presence, perched high and peering low. The song and the beat leaving a longing amongst the stars when quieted. But disruption has caused disturbance. And disturbance has called it from its celestial home once more.

Carrying no more than the power of creation, it prepares to transcend worlds. Like ambers of flame, its movement sparks the interest of all, especially those that would whisper. But nothing stops the eternal being from its quest of ordination. Its quest to discover the new amongst the old.

Blacker than night, more radiant than light, it launches.

Soaring, it peered below and around with disappointment. Another rotation, a new generation. The whispering is as strong a millennia before. On it soared, determined to complete its ordination. Hope in every breath, belief in every beat.

It soared through the air with no limits. A master of the skies, it manipulated each current to reach the unexpected destination. Its distinctive song recognized by all but understood by few danced on the waves as it pierced through.

The night of its feathers glimmered under the sun. Colors from every universe making the feathers home, shown brightly about as the teacher graced the sky. All creation had cinched itself into it, from its soul to its call. It, the embodiment of creation's cycle, darkness birthing color.

The teacher, seated somewhere between heaven and man, had determined to dawn its gift on a worthy soul once again.

The wise mother watched on
as a child came alive.
The wise mother watched on
as a child discovered what was inside.

"Mother, it speaks to me." He smiled.
"Mother, it calls to me."

"Yes, my child. It does," replied the wise
    mother with warmth in her eyes.
"Speak back as it has spoken to you."

So, a child called.
A child sang.
A child ran and jumped
and never wondered if strange.

And the crow replied.
With beauty in its eyes.
The crow discovered
a worthy soul that resides.

The wise mother would let them be.
There, the wise mother would leave them
to their journey.

And the wise mother,
even if unable to hold his hands
coaxed a child gently
to be vigilant as a child becomes a man-child
in the new lands.

And so a child's lessons from the teacher began.
As the wise mother allowed him to stand.
While the defending father quietly built a standard against man.

To be different and free
was a place of plenty.
But to be different and free
would leave a child exposed to many.

III

THE DOORS

The ways we take, reveal.

The crow began a child's journey with haste.
The crow knew a child's time was precious
in this precarious space.
The crow understood what a child would come to learn.
That a child's time is always now.

So, the crow shrouded the sun as it sung.
Darkness not only concealed
but revealed and begun.

Another world appeared.
A dimension of sorts some may say.
Here, in this place, sat forms.
Forms that transported to what soon
      would be known as each way.

Translucent it was in form.
This place could not be held,
it was a place that was beyond norm.

Yet, as elusive as it seemed
it was clearer than any dream.
Each way awaiting to host
any who would come with no sense of
      conquer, no desire to boast.

There a child sat, the crow at hand.
Surrounded was a child by forms with a presence, a command.
Each form an elongated space. Not quite a shape, but
    confined at all sides except atop, going on in infinite.
    Within each of the nine forms hovered an image.

One appeared a dark sphere.
Seeming to breathe and beam with life.
A universe where the dark shown
as bright as light.
Mesmerized if locked in its gaze.
Clearly a power, an ascension, a blaze.

Another an ancient stone-layered triad.
A familiar pattern, a shape.
Encircled by the dust with which a child danced and escaped.
Each stone sitting atop another.
From greater to smaller,
it was Earth from asunder.

In another sat an orb attached to a stem and flat bottom.
Vast was its hollowing.
Deep as a pit.
Atop a finely sharpened line did it sit.
The disk that lay flat
as smooth as shined metal.
Leaving one to wonder if what on top it could handle.

Within another a hook shape a detached circle below.
Fluid like a river did the shape greet you.
Like a drop up from the sea did the circle sit beneath.
Increasing the wonder with every movement, every hover.

Another a living violently swirling series of continuous
    lines, gaping atop and narrowing in descent.
Ominous and haunting they lived without control.
Commanding and daring one to attempt to come and know.
Each line its own pattern, each swirl its own melody.
Its might was its own, it had known no defeat.

In another heavy linked old metal pieces.
As if sitting for ages,
forged by the gods with no design in mind except cages.
Seeming impervious, looking like the weight of a world.
These links were unforgiving.
Not coaxed by magic or pearl.

Another a majestic, winged creature.
Its expanse, massive.
It flown royal and daring.
One wing held the east as the other caressed the west.
Beneath its shadow one could rest.
With each beat all elements relayed
that this creature could not be dismayed.

Floating within another was a burning sphere.
With majesty did it glare.
Knowing no one could maintain against it not a single stare.
Emanating from it an intense energy
but instead of away, pulled towards it everything seemed.
Unmoved and unshaken, it simmered and was a living flame.
Burning came from within, no seeking acclaim.

And within the last floated a solid material,
    smooth and without blemish.
Sleeker than ice.
Behind it darker than night.
Flawless.
No imperfection.
Revealing the hidden things, those endangering true sight.

With the gentility of the first spring breeze,
    the crow would begin to transport a child.

As if in a dream or in a daze, a child would see
    things on display.
Flashes indescribable, but present as the day.

With time the crow flew on,
exposing a child to more.
Still as a dream or daze,
but nurturing the knowing of the Heavens' ways.

All the while were the caressing whispers.
Understanding, the crow moved swiftly against the listeners.

IV

THE WAY OF CREATION

Here is the safest place you'll ever be.
A place of just you and divinity.

In the beginning there was nothing . . .
But darkness.
Are how the stories are told.

But from darkness comes creation.
Everything, the new and the old.

The crow knew all who were different
would walk their own road.
The crow knew all who were different
would walk alone.
So the crow revealed to a child
the state of the gods.
Of darkness that protected
and was the catalyst for truth or facades.

The crow led a child through the dark sphere. Darkness
consumed a child. But this darkness was alive. It pulsed. In it
was an energy . . . it was energy.

In comfort a child found himself in darkness
no matter how bright the sun wished to have shown.
In comfort the child found himself in darkness
because within he realized he was never alone.

The crow knew all who were different
maintained their own glory.
The crow knew all who were different
lived their own history.
So the crow revealed to a child
the power of this station.
Through darkness a child
could birth all creation.

"Witness the home of creators," came the crow.

"The Black?" responded a child.

"The untainted open. Where man sees nothing, creators see limitless opportunity. No restrictions, no notions, boundless creativity."

"But there's nothing here."

"Look again. Man would have you believe that darkness is nothing, but darkness is the birthplace of all life. From darkness springs forth all colors and life.

Release your mind, release yourself. Allow yourself to flow in a space with no parameters, no constructs. A space that is yours for the making.

Create the world you desire, and you take yourself higher."

In this station, a child became a creator. Stillness was his companion, and aloneness was his friend. In this place, in this space, he discovered the compacted colors so tightly woven to form darkness. Darkness was not a void or chasm, but boundless energy.

By pulling the threads he could create all that he could imagine without disruption, without displays, a child could finally play.

Here, a child witnessed the miracle of creation. An explosion of energy. Spirit upon the deep. A sprouting from the Earth. A cry from a womb.

The power and beauty of darkness
shown all about.
A child and the crow's reflection
matched and they danced on the Heavens
with no worry and no doubt.

"Don't forget who you are
all manner of creature.
Creator of worlds
protector of this power,
a beauty beyond steeple.

The night is your skin and sky
the darkness your feature.
There is hard pressed a greater crime
than to eclipse thine self
for the pleasure of a lost people.

Go bold and high,
whether a journey is pleasing.
In the dark sky
your divine energy is made easy."

V

THE WAY OF MYSTERIES

All things are not known.
But what can be, may be revealed.
A life in tune, is a life lived.

Back into the hall a child stepped. Already his evolution beginning to a man-child. A child was not the same. Walking as if the universe knew a child's name, a child moved from the dark without worry of acclaim.

A child approached; the millennial-old rock stood unmoved. Telling stories through the cracks and lines that weaved its body like a tapestry. Entered a child and the teacher into the form with the stone-layered triad. As if the ancient dust knew a tale of former glory, dust swirled about a child with gusto and fury. A child stood, appearing as kissed sweetly by a translucent sun.

"What are mysteries?" asked a child.

"Every song I sing will not be interpreted."

The majestic crow carried on its wings the
    balance of ancient and future time.
The crow was a creature of the divine.
Having traveled the heavens and the earth,
The crow would sharpen a child before a
    child understood its worth.

Into this new place, a child was running to catch, singing to call, and jumping to fly with the crow at every moment. Singing would the crow be. Gracefully moving.

Beating, beating, and beating. The beating of the wings slowly caught the heartbeat of a child, and the spirit of a child began to awaken to the space of the mysteries.

"Mysteries are precious things. They are in front of you, beside you, above you, beneath you, within you. So present are they, but because man has become absorbed in the end, man misses the beauty of universes within. Teachings that exist without questions.

The mysteries bring progress only fathomed while shrouding secrets yet ready to be unearthed. They heal without question, they enlighten, but only when one stills the self."

"Why does the crow fly?" asked a child.

"I am not merely a bird absently moving through the air. But a messenger, a carrier. But even as light as air, I understand there is a time to set and a time to dare.

A being intentionally visiting this place and the other.

A being in tune like no other."

"Why does the tree stand so long?"

"The tree is not a lifeless object standing in the middle of the ground, but an extension of the Greater. The tree is connected to a presence and because of that connectedness, is a giver of life.

Giver of life it may be, the tree understands each season brings its own balance and harmony."

"Why does the wind move?"

"The wind is not a reactionary element. It is not purposed for pleasing.

The wind is the messenger, the mover, and the healing.

Unharnessed and untamed, even the wind recognizes its flow to be guided by the unnamed."

"Why..."

"A child is open. Open to the beauties of the mysteries shown about you. Cherish what a child has come to and with humility be with the mysteries."

So much a child could learn. Slow, but a child could continue
to earn from the mysteries if with openness and humility he
supped with the ancients that others had forsaken. Discovery of
all things to know.

A child had entered into the mysteries
without ever being coaxed.
This space could cause a child to explore.
To question, to seek of the mysteries, to learn more.
The journey of discovery would open the door.
More ways to living, more ways to seeing,
more ways to existing, more ways to being.

The world is big, and the universe endless the crow would reveal to a child. Everything may not be known. But the quest to knowing could be everything. This would blossom in the soul of a child.

Because a child dared to ask *why*, a child dared to explore mysteries, a child dared a different journey, a child would change. Thinking differently would be his standard. Seeing anew would be his norm. Interactions with the universe without right or wrong opened a child to experiences beyond the lore.

With the power of the mysteries a child could evolve, a child could bring change to the world around him.

"Into the mysteries all things flow.
Out of the mysteries all things grow.

No matter the prominence one has established,
    it is the mysteries that remain.
Stay open to the wisdom of the unknown that moves all about you.
Explore true life that is shown to those willing to view.

To wonder is life.
To wander, your might."

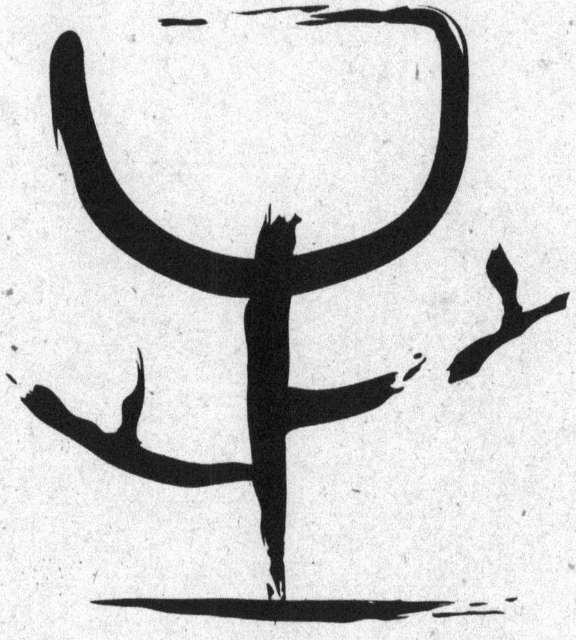

VI

THE WAY OF GROWTH

There is no greater impediment of man than to make a sin of the natural process of evolution.

Returned. To the stillness of the hall. A child more chiseled, forming further into a man-child. The journey was still far from done. And there the crow hovered, above the way which lie an orb affixed to a stem. Through the threshold a child ventured.

Then came the sound of moving water. Seeking, a child ventured closer to the stemmed orb.

"Careful. Do not touch.

One must be ready to welcome evolution and trust."

A child approached with caution. A slight tremble at hand for fear of what lie ahead. But as a child drew closer to moving water, calm rested on his being. He braved to peer on and question his thirsting soul.

What he witnessed he almost could not believe. He stood quietly attempting to understand. Before him, within the stemmed orb water played in a cycle.

Water rose to the very limits. But then as magic released itself into nothingness.

Filled. Released. Filled. Released. Filled. Released.

"All things evolve by flow or by process.

To be in the constant same state is unnatural.

The water from void to nourishment.
Awakening life in all things.

The earth from bare to bountiful.
Nourishing life and love so beautiful.

The tree from sapling to oxygen.
Breathing for the earth and all within to progress.

As the water flows a new into the new, be as the water.

As the earth understands the end and beginning
    of a season, be as the earth.

As the tree understands when it must expand
    or move its roots, be as the tree."

A child stood still—hypnotized. This time not by the water, but the crow. Lifted the crow with nothing in hand. No notion, no worry, no land.

A child still awakening could only understand so much.

The undertaking of more haunting within a child's touch.

"To know more is to want more."

"To want more is to work more."

"To work more is to have more," sung the crow.

"To have more requires more," warned the crow.

So a child gave into the sensation of greater. Desiring to be one with this cycle of filling and releasing. Submitting to his cycle of evolution of being. He released.

A child's body chased the mind,
and the mind the spirit,
and the spirit the soul.

"I am in this place," spoke a child.

"I see this precarious thing. Even in my getting, have I received understanding?

Am I not to be satisfied by the wonders we have already seen?

Is it not my shine to be a lamb?

I have come this way but I find solace in what I am."

And it began. A child's tension to evolve, to see more, to know more, to experience more. Reaching outward beyond what was taught or what held true, a child's spirit hungered for greater.

"*The opposing force to evolution is stagnation. Hidden in plain sight of confidence and comfort.*

You must release, in order to restore.

Man-child wake up,
and slumber no more.
Empty thine cup,
and thirst for more."

VII

THE WAY OF CURIOSITY

"Ask, and it shall be given you.
Seek, and you shall find.
Knock, and it shall be opened unto you."

THE WAY OF
CURIOSITY

In contemplation they entered into the hall.

As a child evolved into a man-child so his spirit began to open to complexities and simplicities of the same. Observing the crow, a man-child contemplated.

Crossed they together through the floating hook and orb. As they moved, the crow launched from its perch upon a child becoming a man-child, a child watched the crow curiously. The crow gliding from one place to the next.

The crow explored with an authority. Seeming detached from any boundaries that may have ever existed. Appearing to discover areas, the crow moved without ceasing.

As if one, a child becoming a man-child moved as the crow. A child becoming a man-child sensed no boundaries. All was to be discovered. Deeper in they went, descent, ascent. All things a universe to know.

To a child everything was nothing and nothing was everything.

This place wade quietly.
Never interfering with a child's curiosity.
A child discovered depths, a child reached through the sky.

A child becoming a man-child and the crow continued to be intwined. Flowing in this place without notion of the right way. With every movement, a new sensation. With every movement, exploration. With every encounter, a child becoming a man-child, evolving.

The constant synchronous dance continued. Leaving no limits in what could be done. No question too far, no movement declared right, no notion of concern, no play undone. The curious spirit only fortified.

Again and again was this harmony displayed.
Again and again foundations laid.

So natural was this way, like a heartbeat. A child becoming a man-child moved into all things. No thing was beyond his reach for without knowing he had learned the flow that is to seek.

"*For a child becoming a man-child everything was nothing and nothing was everything.*

To a child becoming a man-child, ask, to be given. Seek, to find. Knock to be opened. Continue in the legacy of the Divine."

VIII

THE WAY OF
THE UNTAMED

My sweet child, I am all colors in compact.

I have felt the feels, I have called aloud,
I have changed directions, I have ascended clouds.

No matter what space or what time,
I have fully known and been fully known.

For those who truly know the brilliance of my hue,
they have allowed the Source to be untouched
in a world with a singular view.

A man-child sits quietly with his majestic crow.
Time has drawn on him.

"Why is it I feel so long?" asked a child becoming a man-child.

"*Tell me*," responds the crow.

"Is it because I am expected to be a certain way?"

"*Tell me.*"

"Is it because I must control my natural sensation?"

"*Tell me.*"

"Is it because I am to train for a singular destination?

Or have I without hesitation
accepted a singular path as the way to be?
Or have I simply lost my sight to see?"

The crow only ruffled its feathers as it looked towards the way
with violently swirling lines. Energy pulsing, palpable. The
crow, steadfast, gazed at the way. And through the way a child
becoming a man-child traversed hesitantly but seeking to know.

Into a new place, there was a stillness.

An eerie peace never before experienced in any other way.
Rays of light shining from above. Quietly a child becoming
a man-child gazed until disrupted by what lie below.

Pastures destroyed. Pastures fully green. Objects strewn about as
if a mighty stone had been released with fury. Objects standing
as if fixtures in time.

Slowly moving, the crow at hand, a child becoming a man-child
progressed into this place. Moving until stopped by a
sudden shift.

"*An untamed energy. When freed the energy does extraordinary things, both beautiful and terrifying. It moves with petrifying grace. Blind to superficially imposed limits and relentless against unnatural hindrances.*

An untamed energy, a natural force. But observe with grace it touches nothing unnecessary, at all times connected to a source."

A child becoming a man-child looked on in trembling. As forces converged from the Heavens and the earth. As above darkened while this force gathered, he retreated to a covering.

Hidden from its view, a child becoming a man-child looked on frozen. Peering as if looking for his own soul. This force, it moved. Although there was no known destination in view, this force moved to what appeared to be music only it knew.

No path, no signs, no guide, the force moved creating its way. Devastation, felt a child becoming a man-child.

"It is the fullness of this force
that makes it most alluring and powerful.
The fullness it brings on its journey
to overcome all obstacle.

It follows no script,
and is indiscriminate in its time.
It chooses no path,
but it leaves wakes of all kind."

Hearing intently, a child becoming a man-child stared on. The force still moving in its own rhythm and its own terrifying beauty. And then as if called home, the force was gone.

Had he not witnessed it with his own vision, a child becoming a man-child would not have believed it existed. Its form present for but a moment. But even in a moment, the force he would not forget.

Confused with all that appeared and that happened, in a silent whisper a child becoming a man-child questioned,

"What was that to reveal?"

*"And when he was a child,
he thought as a child,
he spoke as a child,
he lived as a child ending in incredible things.*

*A child could create heavenly places
and see devastating things.
If not careful, as he grew and put away childish things,
paths will come into view
and will be paths that all men knew.*

*There is no one way. There is no right path. There is no wrong
direction. There is the journey that exists from moment to moment.
Whether a child becoming a man-child embraces the journey is for
his own determination.*

To go left or go right is not a decision but the beauty of a flickering life. No matter which way a child becoming a man-child journeys, he journeys without hesitation, boundary, or precepts.
He journeys in full might when he journeys without sight.

He journeys connected and without apology. Disciplined in connection to the source guiding his force.

Being, for a child becoming a man-child, lies in the embrace of the untamed living in his days.

There are no mistakes, there are only ways."

IX

THE WAY OF LIBERATION

To bind oneself,
to imprison the soul,
is a power given to only one,
only you possess such control.

In the hall they stood, a child becoming a man-child and the crow. With slow breath and stillness of mind, a child becoming a man-child patiently waited for the revealing of the next way.

The crow made not a sound but the beat of wing against the wind. The crow ascended yet again to reveal the next bend. Without turning back the crow flew, and through the heavy linked old metal pieces, it flew from view.

Heavy. Heavy was this place. A child becoming a man-child could barely move. Looking around he could not make out the crow against the weight. He could not recall how he came to be in this state.

In grief a child becoming a man-child released an exhausted breath. Searching for the crow in desperation.

"What is this?"

"How did this come to be?"

"Swiftly come binds when one loses control. When one forgets the moment, when one is lost in dismay, binding takes over and it starts in the soul."

"But I have done nothing nor said anything. I have not offended another, rather they have done those to me. I have only loved deeply, sometimes to be left alone. I have cared for others sometimes losing my own control.

I have forgone my own to ensure progress for another. I have sat humbly and gave praise to the other.

Do I wish for some things to have been different? Do I look to tomorrow for a brighter day? Of course, but what sin say you to think in this way?"

The crow circled as if capturing prey.

"Speak!

Don't make me suffer.

Give me peace and remove these burdening structures
so I may go free."

The crow circled as if capturing prey.

To the soul the crow spoke.

"*A child becoming a man-child has given permanence permission
to hold him.*

Happenings of yesterday and worries of tomorrow
Constantly blinding from the moment.
The moment which he is ever unable to borrow.

*A child becoming a man-child has given impermanence permission
to adorn him.*

Wearing these burdens so proud and high.
A child becoming a man-child has allowed reality,
    beliefs, and perceptions to set him aside.

A child becoming a man-child has given construct permission to
shelter him.

Built with bricks of systems,
set with the clay of norm.
A foundation made of teachings and logic, a top of conform.

A child becoming a man-child has made burden his rest.

These burdens bit by bit from ground to eye,
linking bit by bit until unable to see the sky.
Allowing cycles, judgment, and fear to materialize,
a child becoming a man-child slowly hunches over,
over, and over until he is paralyzed.

Even still in all these things, a child becoming a man-child
had assumed the things of others' to be.
Others' limits, others' beliefs.
Others' judgments, others' motifs.

But even more wrenching than what others may have dealt,
was the fact that he never realized the true culprit was self."

A child never thought of the next day or the next play.
A child played in the moment, a child seized the day.
"What must be" poured away like oil from the stone.
A child's play was truly his own.

No rules, no do's, no don't's.
No will's, no should's, no won't's.
To the sky set the crow a child's eye
Beyond the sky ventured a child's inner eye.

And as one a child and crow moved
Days had no face, life was pure tune.

And there I was, a child becoming a man-child realized.

"Unfree because of me."

*"You can fly free
release what you cannot control."*

*"You can fly free
remove the removable stole."*

*"You can fly free
come from within unnatural and hidden shelters."*

*"You can fly free
break the haunting tethers."*

After time and time of contemplation.
A child becoming a man-child realized
he was his own liberation.

THE WAY OF FLIGHT

*Would you fly
if you knew your wings?*

Returning to the hall, slowly they re-collected.
The mystical winged creature came into view.
And without turning a child becoming a man-child knew.
This was the next way from teacher to pupil.
So he stepped through barely seeking approval.

Perched high a child becoming a man-child could hardly catch where the ground started. In stillness a child sought the teacher. With earnest heart and thunderous beating, a child plead with his eyes to find the winged creature until his eyes landed and greeted the teacher.

Silence between them. Almost the only thing on which to hold.
A child becoming a man-child watched as the crow prepared.
Spreading of the wings, strengthening of the back,
    attention to the air, and intention in its glare.

A child becoming a man-child watched as the crow ascended
    with each wave, poetically leaving this place with grace.
Nothing in talon.
No fear in sight.
No one to carry.
No thing to fight.

A child becoming a man-child sensed the power of the crow's
flight

and searched in earnest for his same might.

"*Flight begins within.*" He heard the crow in his heart.

"*With a heavy heart you will never begin, you will never start.*"

"*Flight is difference.*
Flight is freedom.
Too precious to hold, it cannot be bought or sold.
The heart's smile,
the mind's salvation,
the soul's revelation.
Flight can carry one through Heaven's station."

In awe a child becoming a man-child
    sensed the crow's experience.
In sky with no inhibition.
Responding to the wind.
Controlling the air.
Moving through the here and there.
Effortlessly flowing in any wake
and beautifully soaring without quiver or quake.
The flight a child becoming a man-child ached in wonder
when his day would come to soar and wander.

Slowly a child becoming a man-child would move without tame.
From within he begin to rise.
Hearing the call of the teacher without name,
a call to one to realize.

"He would know no bounds,
he would carry no weight,
he would listen to his spirit
and each step he would take.
The energy from out within would carry him all about
without a thought of claims that roamed about.

His wings had expanded without effort at all.
He gave no thought to whether he might rise or fall.
He glided between day and night,
wake and dreams.
He felt no burdens.
His spirit was a wild thing.

Alive was a child in all his ways.
The Heavens would be revealed in all his days."

A child becoming a man-child's inner eye was no longer askew.
It had awaked to a different view.

He now knew that flight was his song.
He needed no permission.
Forever he belonged to light and vision.

Swift upon the wind.
Not burdened by a way.
A child becoming a man-child knew no end.
His soul always seized the day.

And the wings that slumbered
suddenly became anew.
And a child becoming a man-child remembered
all at once that he flew.

XI

THE WAY OF POWER

There deep within is what
always will be and always is.

They entered through the way of the burning sphere.

"*And I saw the sun made whole,*" recounted the crow.

"*Causing everything around it to grow.*
I watched in wonder
as all things submitted to its thunder.
All might the sun would pull
no other capable to cool.

And I saw the sun made whole.
Never allowing another
to disrupt the energy.
A soul that blazed with such power.
No whimper, no cower."

The majestic crow saw a child from above.
A child filled with wonder and love.
So perched the crow like a stone on a tower.
And made the call for a child to know power.

And so it was that a child ran with the crow for days.
Thinking it was only a game,
a child was in a haze.
But the crow knew exactly the plan.
To make sure a child did not submit to man.

The crow would display the sun, artist of control.
Being.
Centered.
Giver.
Never pulled to another's lull.

Freely a child followed suit.
Letting nature take its root.
Feeling the pure flame of the sun.
A child basked in his invocation to be one.

Allowing the world to open to him.
A child nurtured all to his beautiful whim.

Without knowing he became of one.
He became centered core,
giving life to others,
never pulled to another's chore.

The crow remembered and beamed.
A sweet memory as sweet as a dream.

Flame he felt once more, as he entered through the door. A child becoming a man-child kissed by the heat of an ancient friend. A friend had not yielded to man.

What beauty to behold that one could be unmovable. Sage from on high. One beyond the sky. Untouchable control that stills the soul.

With tear-stained eye, a child becoming a man-child looked on.

"My friend," he whispered. "My kin."

The sun emanated intensely recognizing the realization.
The sun blazed bright to remind a child becoming
    a man-child of this revelation.

"Bask on. Remember what has been.
Sometimes what you need you've had deep within.
To this power you connected long ago
before the appearance of any ego.
With it you danced, you played, you stayed.
How else could you make it, and not be swayed?"

"Bask on. Remember what has always been.
Reconnect. Re-collect. Know that peace, that is still within.

Unmovable you are.
Kin to the star.
Be true to thine self,
let it take you far."

Kin sup with kin.

"*To be reduced for another*," started the crow on ancient ways.
"*Is to set as a rock for use and throw.*
To be as the sun, most ancient of days, neither touched nor undone,
is to be divine, the master of one's days, and in all ways won.

No hour is known to man
to determine any ultimate plan.
No clever creature can beseech you
without your willingness for it to greet you.

Never forget and never cower.
Kings are ordained by the hour.
But You,
You, my child,
You, are the power."

XII

THE WAY OF YOU

And when your identity has turned to grey.
You'll forever be a clay for display.
And when the spirit of you no longer shines,
less be the world as casualty
of this transgression, of this crime.

So it was, they returned from the sun. The kiss of the heat had yet to retreat. But as he rose there was a glimmer. Revealing another way sending into a child becoming a man-child a shiver.

Still looking to the crow, he awaited a sign, a look, some vision. But the crow soared silently as if in a world of its own. Finally, a child becoming a man-child went through alone.

Quietly. He looked over his shoulder. There was nothing there. He searched, but no crow, no one. In the silence, it felt he could be undone.

One foot in front of the other he began to go. Not knowing where he would take him, but on, slow.

A child becoming a man-child felt the absence. He felt the presence of nothing being there. No sounds, no sights, no forms, just he. One foot in front of the other, he continued to go.

With tear-stained eyes he realized this road he must walk, he must walk it alone. He knew nothing only a sense that his soul required forward he go.

Seized by aloneness he paused,
contemplated whether back was the best cause.
Unknowing of what lie ahead,
in his mind he began to dread.

"Why continue you on?" he said in his head.

"I was far ahead.

I met the sun before the dawn and unleashed the power.

The majesty did greet me unlocking my divine eye.
I remembered what it was to have wings and truly fly.

Had experienced levitation from knowing liberation.

Gave into the moment.
My presence, I'd own it.

Emptying out to be filled with more.
Growth coming to me who desired the more.

Nature is in and out.
It is all about.
I am it and it is me.
Together we are we.
Learn from it life's wonders.
Learn from it and not be taken under.

Curiosity sublime.
Seeking, knowing, asking so what would be revealed
     would be revealed in time.

Cradled I in the bosom of creativity.
Supping at the table of divinity.

Patient and steadfast I have been,
only to be alone in the end."

As he moved on, on came a glimmer.
In the middle of nothing causing a shiver.

With caution he proceeded
to fear he never heeded.
On through the space,
he approached in caution.
And alone there it was
his face and no option.

His breath stricken as his heart quickened.

"What is this place?"

He never looked up, never turned his head round
when with age-old grace came the sweet familiar sound.

"Even this, I showed you the divine.

No need to gather from here or there.
No need to wait for things to share,
of beauty and strength always there.
You are the wonder, always dare.

No power can reside,
where within,
the soul one cannot find.

Even then, I saw you a child from high.

Providing you ways.
Giving you the simplest displays.
Only to remind you of the real true.
In the end, the Divine . . . is You."

XIII

THE WHISPERS

It is swifter than slumber.
Its beauty a wonder.

Lightly each foot touched down. The first followed gently by the second. A child becoming a man-child could barely sense gravity. The crow looked on from its perch on high. No stranger to the way, the crow allowed it to sink into a child becoming a man-child.

With nature his teacher
every manner of creature
sought the soul
with the impervious glow.

Still in contemplation he began to sway. Rhythmically left, slowly right, a child becoming a man-child moved as if attuned to a different frequency.

Like a distant song it caressed the edges of his soul. Not too close, barely able to be beheld. Fluid its presence came. It had no introduction; it sought no acclaim.

A child becoming a man-child swayed. In the presence of Whispers he edged on and obeyed. Gently pouring fourth as liquid from a dream, to him it felt like peace and serene.

On it came no end in sight. On it came with a different might.

All at once his spirit rested as the lulls grew on and further manifested.

"Pursue the same.
Only seek more of what has a name." It prodded softly.

"How noble it is to be grateful and content,
to not make a sound,
to take what is sent.
What relief shall there be to not have a question.
To simply enjoy sublime given direction.
With love We come so you need no election.
Peace, shall you have as you live in our correction.
For lined with gold soon you shall see
is to stay in Our presence, to praise Our company.

Remain in place and you will be fine.
Lay in this space
and life can be divine."

He remained with his body relaxed.

Vision askew and all senses dimmed.

A child becoming a man-child seemed to have found his fill.

The crow looked from its perch on high.

The crow said not one thing as if saying goodbye.

"The sky is the limit. The goal is the gold.

What privilege to be where you are.

Right here he twinkles,

Our child is a star.

Rest your mind, stay a while.

All you need is within this mile.

You need not worry or even guess.

The road we offer is for only the best.

Lay your roots and build sky high.

For the sky is the limit and to it We'll fly.

Come and be one.

From you nothing will be hidden.

Come and be one.

All will be given.

A gentle breeze grazed his face. The crow ascended, still not a sound, but a child becoming a man-child's soul recognized the blow. A slight disruption in the refrain. The soul reached out for what it once knew, struggling through the many somethings held true.

The crow sensed the stirring,
the seeking from a distant view.
So delicately the crow began calling
to a child it always knew.

From an unknowable distance he felt a calling.
Even though through senses his being was falling.

"Why didn't you let me know?!" Quiet tears and still pain.

"If I had, how would you grow?"

"The greatest way is in you.
But in order to get there
you must traverse what things will come
to become one with what's true.

I do not know each moment of your days.
I have not come to deprive you of your journey.
Only to enlighten you that you are the key to your story.

The real victor is the one who
maintains the self amidst the Whisper.
The one to see through,
and know divine against reaper."

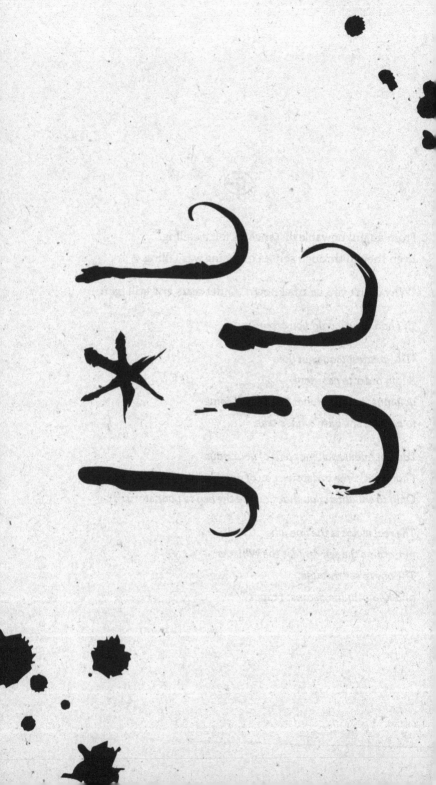

EPILOGUE

THE WIND

Love ,
no blemish I see.

Trust,
learnings are nothing before Me.

Be,
not of thyself, but as One, for I Am thee.

A gentle breeze whisked away the Whispers.
Coming from a familiar unnamable origin.
What could only be the indivisible, the
      Source, coming to let flow, again.
A child becoming a man-child, relented, his
      soul naked from the course.
No longer of the mind,
tears staining the heart and washing behind,
in comfort, he, with crow steady beside,
released into the love of the Divine.

The Wind had a subtle beauty, a grace.
Its movement, poetic.
Its presence, magnetic.
Before it, all time erased.

Warmth indescribable.
Surrounding, comfort untold.
A gentle salve for the battered,
a balm for the soul.

Like returning from days' journey.
Like never being alone.
Untouchably all around thee.
The Wind, a love of its own.

Flowers never knew a scent.
The sun not touching its light.
The ocean un-containing.
Its power deeper than night.

Call home the Wind would.
Call home the livened soul.
Call home the Wind would.
Call home to be with and know.

A child understood,
that to It he always belonged.
Released he to It,
the origin of song.

The Wind could move mountains and carry seas.
A child somehow knew
and never wondered at the ease.
The Wind, a gentle power acknowledged by all the hours.
A child never resisted
and so was carried by its powers.

Quietly the crow looked on. A child becoming a man-child not
aware of its presence.

In peace the crow observed a child becoming a man-child
flowing with the Essence.

A child was with joy a beautiful scene
as a child sent his love and play as an offering.
A child with splendor and so serene
was alive to make the Wind ring.

Steadily the crow appeared with the Wind in communion.
The crow and Wind were a union.
The crow would demonstrate its ways for a child to channel.
Movement that was innate, having no resistance or no battle.

A child becoming a man-child had not moved.
Met by an old friend,
he transported to another time, to another space,
 a place without and within.

Quietly the crow looked on. A child becoming a
 man-child not aware of its presence.
In peace the crow observed a child becoming a
 man-child flowing in the Essence.

The crow would release what's home with calm and ease.
Recognizing that true home is all creation and divinity.

The crow would clear its vision to be ready and to hear.
Knowing sight is essential to revelation, wandering without fear.

The crow would check for the feel of the breeze.
Essential it is to be One with the Heavens and nature,
to be beyond the perceived.

The crow would step with courage.
Prepared to release all known,
to gain all from this flight, to sing its true song.

The crow would check for the feeling from above.
Revealing its Present is in tune with the Divine.

The crow would rouse its feathers freeing all things.
Ready for each obstacle that comes to force its land,
so with grace it shall move beyond plan.

The crow would take pause and steady the heart.
It knew no journey could it take,
if the heart held to what it could not take.

The crow would flex its wing and talon.
Understanding that sensing Oneself increases the center,
    preventing relenting or cower.
Allowing the crow not to be hurled to and fro,
but to be the power.

The crow would extend all of its being.
Flight is not possible if the self its not seeing.
Flight is not possible if the self it confuses with being.

The crow would be carried by the Powerful and not leading.

A child would see this for so many days.
A child would see this and not wonder, but gaze.
A part of him it would naturally be.
A prime in readying for each cycle, each journey.

With the wise mother and defending father,
a child was and did not falter.
Covered by beauty and raise,
a child was protected from the haze.

All had come together for a child to wander.
For a child to be.
To experience.
To thunder.

To himself he came. A child becoming a man-child remembered
what it was to be love and be loved. He sensed the presence of
the Essence, and welcomed it in. A child becoming a man-child
began to know that whatever the cycle, if he remembers the
connecting ways, himself he could be for all his days.

Lowered the crow
with the Wind in tow
and sang so delicately.
It was to a man-child
the natural melody.

"No day is the same.
Each way can lay claim.

In time you will see,
these ways accompany thee.

It's the power inside you
that will always guide you.

It's the sacred Wind
that dwells with and in.

Release yourself from what you never belonged.
And again
be with the Wind
as your being, It's in.

The comfort and carry, It will eternally be.
If ever you are lost, return to the ways for
the Wind to again carry thee."

FLOWERS

This piece is not a product of me, but a flowing through a channel of openness. I am grateful to be open enough to experience and share. But through this lifetime of experience and three-year process of channeling and materializing, I have had enumerable supports. This acknowledgment is only a hint of the flowers that I owe and are specific to the journey in manifesting this piece.

Mom, thank you for being the seeing, advancing, and knowing force in my life. Thank you for opening my spirit and encouraging me to fly. Thank you for standing at each side of me as ways manifested themselves before me and in my wake. Thank you for being a pillar by day and night. Thank you for walking with me through the fray. And thank you for carrying me in my worst of days. Thank you for being the epitome of unconditional love.

Dad, thank you for being the open, accepting, and defending force in my life. Thank you for protecting my spirit and normalizing my ability to fly. Thank you for not seeing anything as a surprise but as a natural evolutionary step in my journey. Thank you for showing me what it is to walk in constant self-grace. Thank you for being the epitome of unconditional love. I hope the winds carry my love to you everywhere you are.

Azul, thank you for joining my journey. Thank you for seeing something beyond the present. Thank you for not settling. Thank you for brutal honesty. Thank you for permission. Thank you for creating space. Thank you for being a guide through this literary process. Thank you for diving headfirst into an unknown and drawing me through the same. Thank you for becoming a friend. Thank you for recognizing the crow.

Sheri, thank you for reading four infant lines on a whim on a street in King-Lincoln Bronzeville, in 2019. "You've got to put this out," words that rung in my heart since that moment, along with so many other unbelievably beautiful sentiments. Thank you for setting a gentle siren call that would stay with me in this journey.

Big, thank you for sacred moments. Thank you for choosing to use your time to sup with me in conception. When there were no words, and only concepts, only images, thank you for seeing through to another side. Thank you for holding space for me to release. Thank you for requiring that I move forward.

Prince, thank you for not catching a breath before pushing me forward into this work. Thank you for being unforgiving in believing there is space for me, for this piece, in this world. Thank you for choosing to use your time to read this piece, for experiencing this piece, and for sharing with me during the early stages of this piece.

Renee, thank you for believing this to be my natural path. Thank you for lifting me in my doubt. Thank you for reading any passage, any iteration, and always sewing light for me to move forward. Thank you for feeling the clouds with me, but making room for and reminding me of the light.

Aureyl, thank you for intentionally creating space for this piece to materialize. Thank you for knowing exactly how to move me forward. Thank you for knowing how to bring me back to this space to finish this work after extensive time away. Thank you for seeing where I could no longer. Thank you for being a wind for wings, a chord for song, a place to belong. Thank you for being unrelenting. Thank you for reminding. Thank you for being my love.

Thank you to Rockrose Press for trying something new. Thank you to the entire team that took moments in their lives to bring this piece into existence. Thank you for being honest, for being sincere, for being present with me.

Thank you to all the incredible souls, which would require another book of its own for me to thank, who have been a part of me coming to this place and creating a beautiful journey in this life.

May you all know beauty for all your days. May you all never lose to dismay. May you all choose to experience the glory in each of your ways.

Thank you to the Heavens above for the constant grace bestowed upon me. Thank you for all that is, was, and is to come.

Thank you to my crow. Thank you for comforting me from my youth, to this day. May our companionship grow even more wildly as we dare to touch Heaven and earth . . . together.

ABOUT THE AUTHOR

STEFAN T. WONG, born in Columbus, OH, has been described as a contrarian, an enigma. From homelessness to growing up on S. 22nd St "Deuce Deuce," he has journeyed a path affording him to share space with and consult political leaders, religious leaders, executives and entrepreneurs of multi-million-dollar enterprises, and award-winning artists. He has been recognized as a *Future History Maker* by UrbanOne Radio, tapped as a seminal brand ambassador for the Greater Columbus Arts Council's Emmy-nominated City of Columbus' Art Makes Columbus Campaign, and recognized by SuperLawyers and Who's Who.

Visit him online at www.stefantwong.com.

Printed in the USA
CPSIA information can be obtained
at www.ICGtesting.com
LVHW030834111123
763363LV00087B/67/J